Published by
Armadillo Books
an imprint of
Bookmart Limited
Registered Number 2372865
Trading as Bookmart Limited
Blaby Road
Wigston
Leicestershire LE18 4SE

ISBN 1-84322-167-5

10 9 8 7 6 5 4 3 2

Produced for
Bookmart Limited by
Nicola Baxter
PO Box 215,
Framingham Earl
Norwich NR14 7UR

Designer: Amanda Hawkes
Production designer: Amy Barton

Printed in China

Starting to read – it's perfect!

The not-so-perfect ballerina in this story helps to make sharing books at home successful and enjoyable. The book can be used in several ways to help beginning readers gain confidence.

You could start by reading the illustrated words at the edge of each lefthand page with your child. Have fun trying to spot the same words in the story itself.

All the words on the righthand page have already been met on the facing page. Help your child to read these by pointing out words and groups of words already met.

Finally, all the illustrated words can be found at the end of the book. Enjoy checking all the words you can both read!

The not so Perfect Ballerina

Written by Nicola Baxter · Illustrated by Pauline Siewert

ARMADILLO

Laura loves to dance.

She puts on
her pretty dress.

dress

shoes

She ties her
ballet shoes.

She makes
her hair tidy.

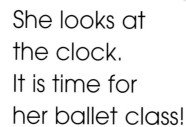

hair

She looks at
the clock.
It is time for
her ballet class!

clock

Laura loves her ballet class!

teacher

beads

stick

hand

Laura's teacher is waiting.

She wears gold beads and carries a stick.

She waves her hand grandly.

"Begin!" she calls. "And dance until I say 'Stop!'"

Laura begins to dance.

The teacher waves her stick. "Stop!"

arm

leg

vase

flowers

But Laura lifts her arm.
Crash!

She lifts her leg.
Ouch!

She twirls and knocks over
a vase of flowers.

"Stop!" cries the teacher
again. "Stop dancing!"

Laura knocks over the teacher!

feet

chair

Laura helps her teacher to her feet and finds her a chair.

"Let's begin again," says the teacher. "Slowly this time!"

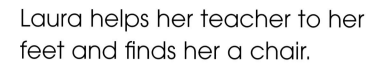

water

But Laura slips on some water on the floor and bumps her bottom!

Ow!

She slides across the floor...

floor

Laura bumps the teacher again!

sofa

"Laura! Please be careful!" says the teacher.

Laura helps her teacher to the sofa. Then she begins to dance very, very slowly.

eyes

The teacher closes her eyes. She falls asleep on a cushion!

cushion

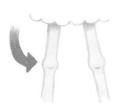

knees

Laura dances more quickly. She bends her knees. Ooops!

She falls on the teacher!

window

door

wall

ankle

"My beads are broken!" cries the teacher. "They are rolling all over the floor!"

"I'll get them!" says Laura.

But the beads make her slip.

Laura bumps into the window.

She bumps into the door.

She bumps into the wall.

"Ow!" cries Laura. "My ankle! It is hurting!"

"Is it broken?" asks her teacher.

grapes

sweets

book

ballerina

The ankle is not broken, but Laura must rest it.

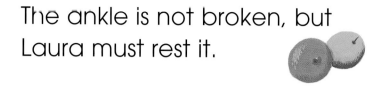

Her teacher comes to see her.

She brings grapes.
She brings sweets.
She brings a book called
How To Be A Perfect Ballerina.

"Don't worry, Laura," she says.
"I have mended my beads.
I have mended my vase.
You can just rest."

"My ankle will soon be mended," says Laura.

"Soon I can be a
perfect ballerina, too!"

Picture dictionary

Now you can read these words!

ankle	arm	beads
book	chair	clock
cushion	door	dress
eyes	feet	floor

flowers

grapes

hair

hand

knees

leg

shoes

sofa

stick

sweets

teacher

vase

wall

water

window

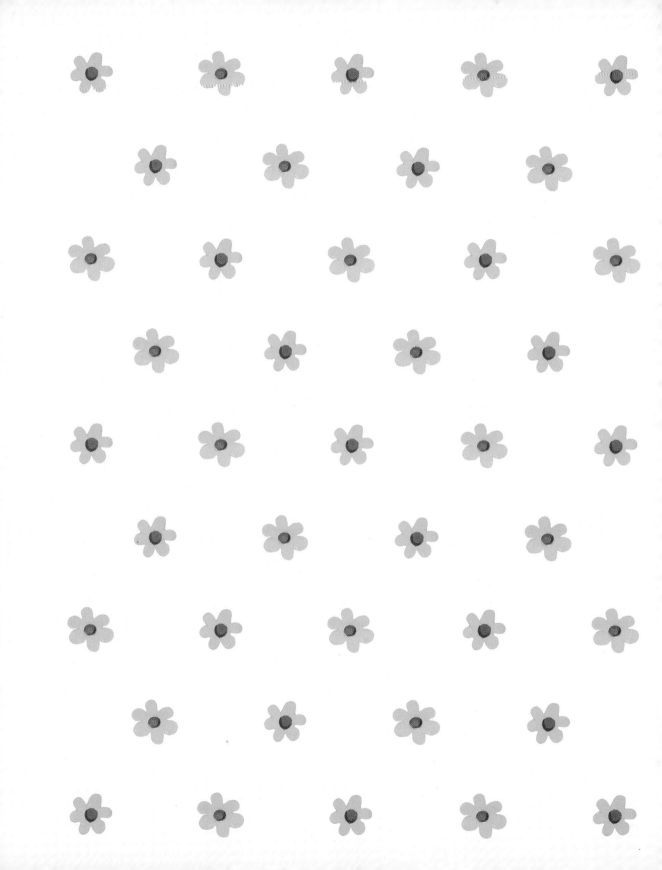